This book is brought to you by CyberSecurity NonProfit (CSNP), a 501(c)(3) nonprofit organization that empowers our community through inclusive and accessible cybersecurity education, awareness, and exploration. Visit us to learn more at CSNP.org!

In a world of data,

Where shadows would loom,

Lived a hacker,

Navigating through gloom.

"Goodnight Moon,"

They'd say with a smirk,

But tonight,

It's "Goodnight Hacker,"

Ready to work.

Beneath the night sky,
A hacker's realm unfolds,
Nocturnal coder, where
Digital mysteries are untold.

Goodnight keyboard,
Keys dancing fast,
Unraveling networks with a
Clickity-clack.

Goodnight coffee,
In the coder's hand tight,
Hacker's companion,
Scripting through the night.

Goodnight rubber duck,
Yellow and wise,
In debugging's dance, your
Conversation helps analyze.

Goodnight exploits,
Stealthy and smart,
Crafting mischief,
With a hacker's heart.

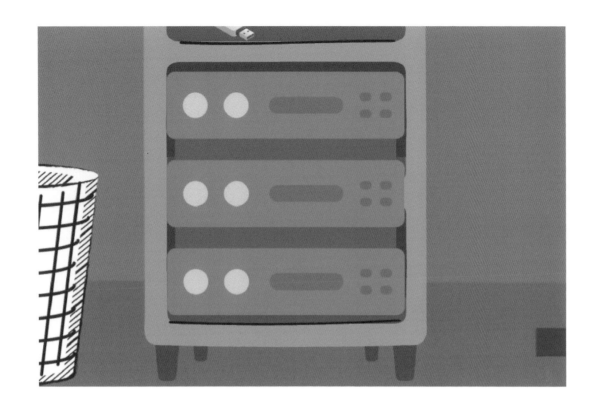

Goodnight server
In the hacker's lair,
Humming while exploits
Take to the air.

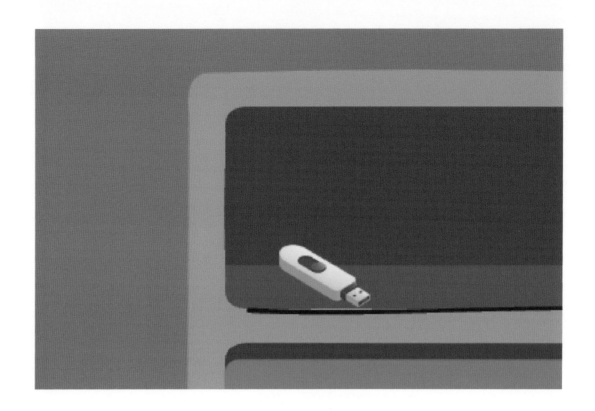

Goodnight USB drive,
So sleek and small,
With hidden malware,
You infiltrate them all.

Goodnight beanbag chair,
Where thoughts take their flight,
In the glow of the screen,
Through the cybernight.

Goodnight sneaky cat,
Agile and sly,
Guarding secrets,
With an observant eye.

Goodnight pizza box,
A feast by their side,
Fueling their code,
In the quiet they ride.

Goodnight black hat,
A mischievous sprite,
Testing defenses,
Lurking in the night.

Goodnight red hat,
A balancing act,
Treading ethical lines,
Avoiding the trap.

Goodnight white hat,
In honor you tread,
Defending systems,
Secure ahead!

And on the wall,

A master of the trade,

A white hat hacker's portrait,

Their skills displayed.

So Goodnight exploits,
And Goodnight rubber duck.

Goodnight bean bag chair,
And Goodnight pizza box.

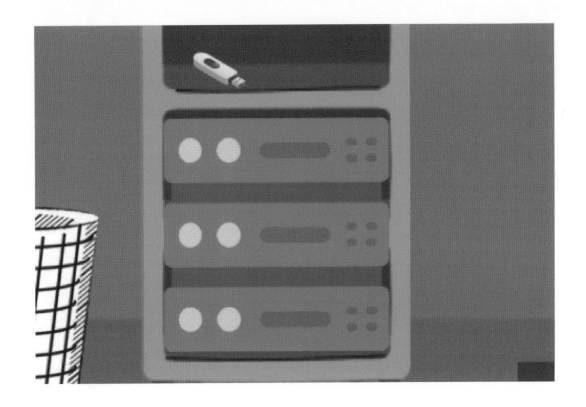

Goodnight server,
And Goodnight USB drive.

Goodnight hackers,
Everywhere you hide.

So Goodnight Moon,
And all you've shown,
Goodnight dear hackers,
Till night is flown.
With dreams of code and
Systems to tame,
Embrace the challenges,
In the hacker's game.

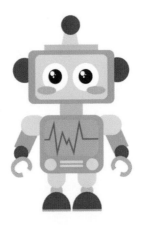

Printed in Great Britain
by Amazon

31453865R00016